UNDER THE GREEN WILLOW

BY ELIZABETH COATSWORTH
ETCHINGS BY JANINA DOMANSKA

THE MACMILLAN COMPANY | NEW YORK
COLLIER-MACMILLAN LTD. | LONDON

The book is printed by offset in four preseparated colors.
An etching was prepared for the key color, dark olive-green.
The other colors—yellow, light green and bright yellow-green—
were each done on an overlay in brush-and-ink and pencil.
The typeface used throughout is Dominante. The title
was set in an old wood type called Jenny Lind.

The Macmillan Company, 866 Third Avenue, New York, New York 10022
Collier-Macmillan Canada, Ltd., Toronto, Ontario

Library of Congress Catalog Card Number: 73-123131

10   9   8   7   6   5   4   3   2   1

To Susan
with love

There is a place I know,

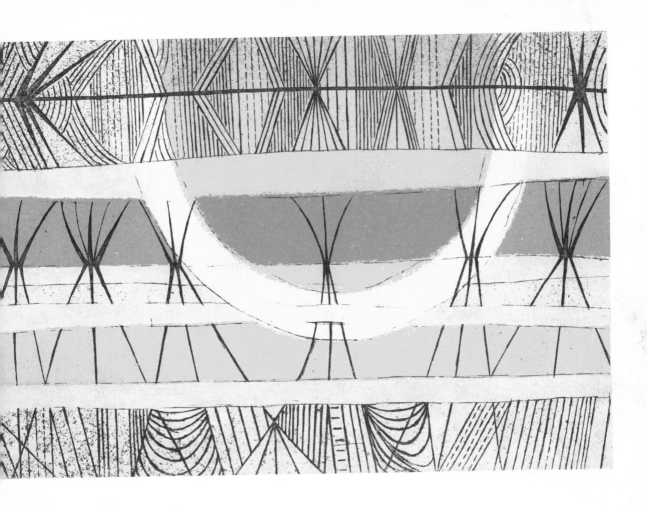

says the sun,

where ducks

and ducklings,

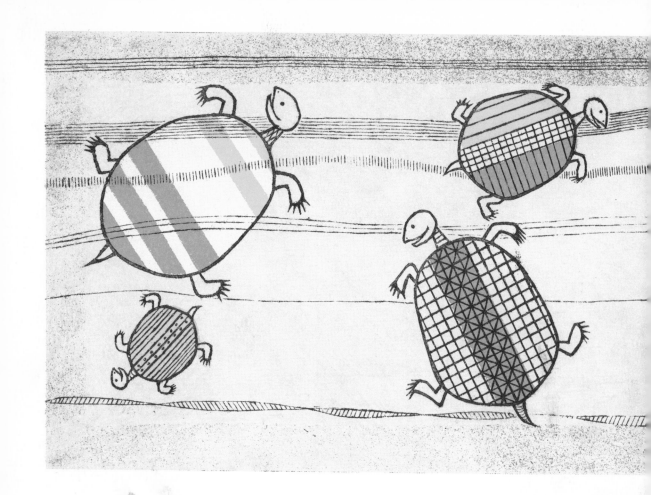

turtles,

trout,

catfish with whiskers,

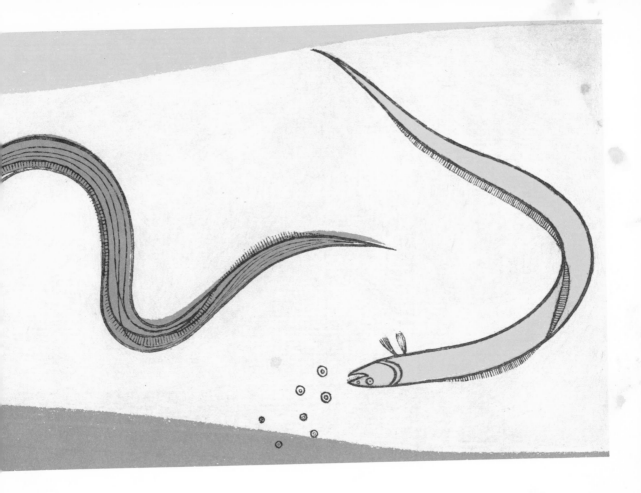

and young eels,

all crowd together in the water

under a willow tree waiting for crumbs.

The ducks kick

the turtles out of the way,

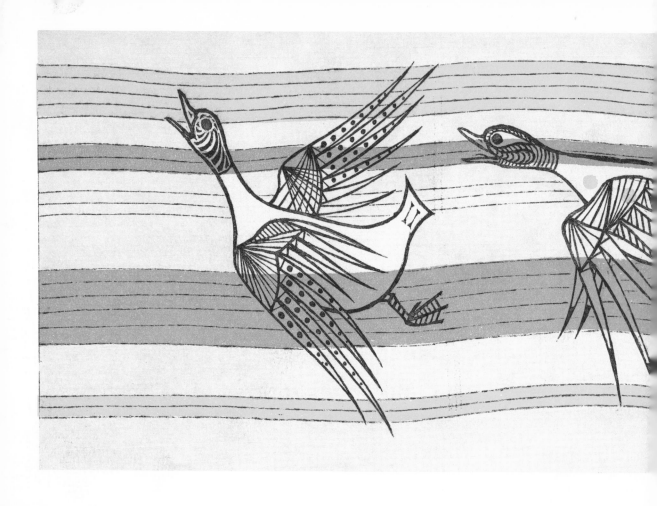

the catfish bite

the ducks' toes,

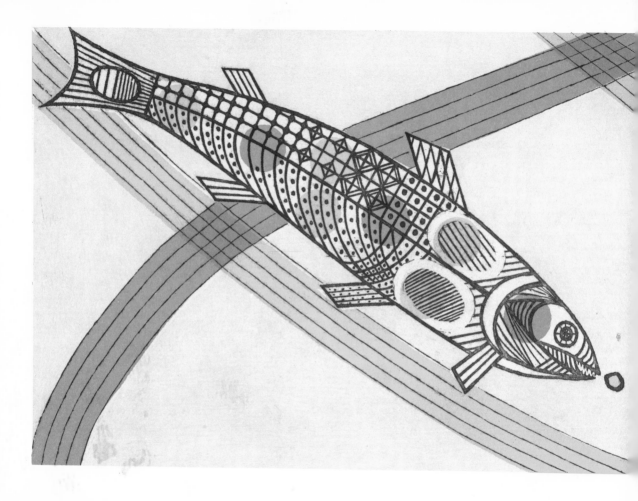

the trout whisk a crumb away

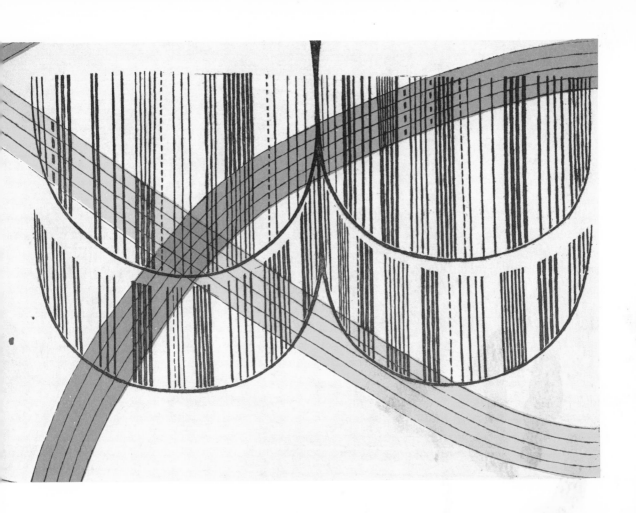

before the others see it,

the little eels try to take

the food out of the turtles' horny beaks.

There they all are,

in the clear water, under the green willow.